Tales of Hindu Gods and Goddesses

Divya Jain

Illustrated by:
Ajay Kumar

ISBN 978-81-7806-195-5

© Unicorn Books
F-2/16, Ansari Road, Daryaganj,
New Delhi-110002
Website: www.unicornbooks.in
E-mail: info@unicornbooks.in

Contents

BRAHMA

*H*induism speaks of three main gods who form what is called the Hindu Triad or Hindu Trinity. They are Brahma, Vishnu and Shiva.

Brahma is the god of creation. His idol shows him with four heads and four arms. In his hands, he holds a drinking vessel (*kamandal*), *kusa* grass, a rosary and a book.

The four heads facing the four directions, represent the four Vedas (Rig Veda, Sama Veda, Yajur Veda, Atharva Veda), the four Yugas (epochs of time—Satya, Treta, Dwapar and Kali) and the four castes (Brahmanas, Kshatriyas, Vaisyas, Sudras). Usually the faces have beards and the eyes are closed in meditation. His consort is Sarasvati, the goddess of knowledge, and his *vahana* (vehicle) is a swan.

It is believed that Brahma was born from a lotus arising from the navel of Lord Vishnu. His abode is called Brahmaloka.

He is also known as Svayambhu (self-born first person), Prajapati (lord of the progeny), Lokesa (master of the worlds), Nabhija (navel born) and Dhatr (sustainer).

Though Lord Brahma is considered the creator of this world and all the people in it, he is not revered in any Hindu temple. In fact, in the whole of India, there is only one temple dedicated to him. There is a very interesting story behind it.

The Curse

Once, the gods decided to carry out a great sacrifice. It was to be for the benefit and vitality of the three worlds (heaven, hell and earth). The sacrifice which was to be especially advantageous to earth, was to be carried out by Lord Brahma. Its successful completion was to bring prosperity and rain showers on earth. 'I have to find an appropriate place to conduct this sacrifice,' thought Brahma.

His search took him to the forests near Pushkar. As he walked into the forest, the trees recognised him. They shook their branches, showering him with flowers.

Brahma was very pleased by the gesture and chose Pushkar as the site for the sacrifice. Immediately, a pool of water emerged and a lake called 'Brahma Lake' was formed. To protect the site from demons, Brahma created four hills in the four different directions – Nilgiri (North), Ratnagiri (South), Suryagiri (East) and Sonchooda (West). Great preparations were made for the sacrifice (*yagya*).

Gods, sages and holy men gathered in large numbers at the appointed day and time. To guard the sacrifice, many gods positioned themselves on these hills. Everything was set to start the sacrifice, but for a major hitch – Sarasvati, the consort of Brahma was nowhere to be seen.

"Where is Sarasvati?" enquired a god. "It is time to make the offerings. As per Hindu rites, both husband and wife have to make oblations in the sacrificial fire."

Lord Brahma sent a priest to call her.

"I am still in the process of getting ready. The wives of other gods and holy men have also not come. It will look odd if I enter the assembly alone. Some household affairs also need to be sorted out. I will come in a while," said Sarasvati.

The priest returned and gave her message to Brahma.

"Sire, we must start with the proceedings. It's getting late," reminded another priest. "The auspicious time period will soon be over and then the efforts put in by everyone will go waste."

"Yes, yes, you are right," agreed an irritated Brahma.

"But unless you have a wife by your side, the rites will be of no use," reminded a god.

Brahma was very angry by the irresponsible behaviour of Sarasvati. Seeing to the need of the situation, he called upon Indra, the god of heaven.

"Indra! Go and find me a wife from wherever you can," ordered Brahma.

Indra hastened. He saw a beautiful young milkmaid carrying a jar of butter.

"What's your name?" asked Indra.

"Gayatri," replied the maiden shyly.

"Come with me immediately," he said and brought her to the assembly. Vishnu and Shiva gave her away in marriage and Gayatri thus became the second wife of Brahma.

"Gods and holy sages, continue with the sacrifice," commanded Brahma, "Gayatri will now become the mother of the Vedas and bring purity to the three worlds."

Accompanied by Parvati and Lakshmi, Sarasvati came to the place of the sacrifice. When she saw Gayatri dressed in bridal clothes, sitting next to her husband, she was mad with anger.

"Oh Brahma! You have rejected me and married another woman! Have you no shame? You have humiliated me in front of everyone! I can't show my

face to anyone! How dare you insult me like this!" raged Sarasvati.

Brahma tried to explain the situation to Sarasvati and asked her to forgive him. But she was in no mood to listen.

"By the powers that I have acquired by doing penance and meditation, I hereby curse you – Brahma! You will never be worshipped in any temple or sacred place other than Pushkar!" proclaimed Sarasvati.

She then pronounced a curse on Indra, Vishnu and Shiva as well, because they had helped Brahma get married. In a huff, she left the assembly

accompanied by Lakshmi and the other goddesses. After a while, they expressed their desire to return.

"In my moment of need, you are deserting me!" cried Sarasvati.

Seething with anger, she again pronounced a curse.

"O Lakshmi! Since you are forsaking me, may you never remain stationary! From now you will dwell not just with the worthy and the just, but also with the wicked, the depraved, the sinful and the immoral!"

Sarasvati then proceeded to Mount Ratnagiri and disappeared into the mountain. At that very place, a small cascade of water gushed out. Later, a temple dedicated to Sarasvati was built there.

But ever since, no prayers are offered to Brahma in any temple.

*Situated in Rajasthan, **Pushkar** is about 11 km west of Ajmer. It's the only place in India, which has a temple enshrining an idol of Lord Brahma. It's also the site of a famous fair by the same name held on Kartika Purnima (full moon day in the month of Kartik). Though animal trading is the main feature of this fair, people throng in large numbers to take a dip in the holy waters of the 'Brahma Lake'. After the dip, they visit the temple and pay homage to the silver-eyed idol of Lord Brahma.*

VISHNU

$\mathcal{L}$ord Vishnu is the god of Preservation. Having a dark bluish complexion, he is often depicted resting on the coils of the thousand-headed serpent Shesh (Anant), who is floating in the waters of the ocean Kshirsagar (ocean of milk).

In his four hands, Lord Vishnu holds a lotus, a mace (*gada*), a conch shell and a discus. His four arms represent the four directions (North, South, East, West). He wears the Kaustubh, a precious jewel around his neck. He is shown dressed in yellow robes and his abode is called Vaikunth.

His *vahana* is Garuda, the eagle. Lord Vishnu's consort is Lakshmi, the goddess of Prosperity. He is known by almost a thousand other names of which Vishvamvar (protector of

Matsya Avatar

Kurma Avatara

Varaha Avatara

Narsimha Avata

the world), Narayan (supreme god), Hari (the saviour) and Swayambhu (self-existent) are very popular.

Lord Vishnu is supposed to be responsible for the sustenance, protection and maintenance of the universe. Whenever any great calamity took place or any of the world's inhabitants became too wicked, Vishnu as Preserver came to earth in some form to help. Once the work was done, he again returned to the skies.

One can't be certain of the exact number of Lord Vishnu's incarnations. The Bhagvad Purana mentions 22 avatars but the best known and accepted avatars are ten in number. All the avatars have an interesting story associated with them. Did you know that once Lord Vishnu transformed himself into a tortise. Would you like to know why? .... Read on.

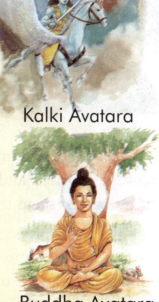

Kalki Avatara

Buddha Avatara

Krishna Avatara

Vamana Avatara   Parasurama Avatara   Shri Rama Avatara

CHURNING THE OCEAN

*O*wing to a curse by a holy sage, Indra, the god of heaven, lost all his powers. Worried and scared, the gods approached Brahma for help, who in turn directed them to Vishnu.

"O Lord, please help us," pleaded the gods, "Due to the curse on Indra, we have all become weak. If the demons get to know about this, they will immediately attack us and take custody of our abode—heaven."

"Hmmm… there is a way out," said Lord Vishnu, "If you drink *amrit* (nectar), not only will you regain your powers, but will also become immortal." The gods listened carefully.

"To obtain *amrit*, you will have to churn the Kshirsagar. But churning that mighty ocean is not an easy task. The joint strength of demons and gods will be required to do that."

The gods approached the king of demons for assistance, who agreed on the condition that gods share the *amrit* with the demons. After this temporary truce, the task on hand was to find a suitable churning pole and rope.

Lord Vishnu advised them to use Mount Mandar as the churning stick and the serpent Vasuki as the churning rope. The next problem was of uprooting Mount Mandar. And this was by no means easy! The huge mountain was over 12300 km high, with roots that went an equal distance into the earth. Lord Vishnu sent his snake Anant, who successfully carried out the task. After this, Vasuki wrapped itself around Mandar and it was placed in the middle of the Kshirsagar.

As suggested by Lord Vishnu, the gods grasped the serpent's tail. The demons then, had to hold Vasuki's head. The process of churning began.

WHIRL! SWIRL! WHOOSH! SWOOSH!
WHIRL! SWIRL! WHOOSH! SWOOSH!

Poor Vasuki's body was tugged and pulled. In distress, he breathed out poisonous fumes and fire. The demons were in great discomfort since they were

holding the snake's head. But in the hope of obtaining the *amrit*, they continued to endure the ordeal.

Soon another problem came up. To churn the ocean, the heavy mountain was revolving at a very high speed. This constant churning pierced a hole right through the bottom of the earth. It was imperative to steady the mountain and prevent it from sinking; else earth itself would be destroyed. In this moment of crisis, everyone again turned to Vishnu.

"O Lord, please help," pleaded the gods once again. "If Mandar is not given a steady base, it will sink down to hell. Years of effort and toil will go waste."

Lord Vishnu smiled and said, "Before starting any auspicious work, one must pray to Lord Ganesha. Since you all forgot to do that, all these problems are cropping up."

"We'll do the needful right away," said the gods in unison and got busy in offering prayers to Ganesha. In the meantime, Lord Vishnu transformed himself into a huge tortoise – Kurma Avatar. He stepped into the ocean and placed the mountain on his hard back.

WHIRL! SWIRL! WHOOSH! SWOOSH!

WHIRL! SWIRL! WHOOSH! SWOOSH!

The churning process was restarted. The gods and the demons continued like this for more than a thousand years, but still there was no sign of the *amrit* emerging from the ocean.

Again Lord Vishnu provided assistance. With his thousand arms, he churned the ocean from not one, but both the sides. So great was the power of Vishnu that he carried out with ease the dual task of supporting a mountain and churning a mighty ocean. Gradually many wonderful objects started emerging.

When finally the *amrit* appeared, there was a great scramble for it. The demons and the gods started fighting over it. For days together they battled. Yet again, Lord Vishnu came forth to help. Transforming himself into a beautiful woman named Mohini, he tricked the demons in such a way that the gods managed to get the entire share of the *amrit*. The gods became immortal and chased the demons away who fled for dear life and escaped to *Patal Lok*.

*The **Kurmanath Swamy Temple** situated in northern Andhra Pradesh is the only temple in India dedicated to Lord Vishnu's second incarnation – the Kurma avatar. It is located in the town of Srikakulam, about 120 km from Vishakhapatnam. This ancient temple has rock edicts from the 11th century AD on its walls. Devotees believe that they'll be absolved of their sins and freed from the cycle of birth and rebirth if they pray here. The temple's shape is like that of a tortoise too!*

SHIVA

Lord Shiva is the god of destruction. He is the last deity of the trinity. He is mostly depicted sitting cross-legged in a yogic position. He has four arms, three eyes and long matted hair. In two arms he holds a *trishul* (trident) and a *damru* (hand drum).

The three eyes represent sun (light), moon (life) and heat. It's a popular belief that Lord Shiva opens his third eye when he is angry.

He wears a crescent-shaped moon on his forehead and snakes around his neck. It is believed that the sacred river Ganga flows down from his hair. His body is smeared with ashes and his abode is Mount Kailash in the Himalayas. In temples he's worshipped not as an icon but in the form of *linga*.

He is also known as Mahayogi (god of ascetism), Nataraja (god of dance), Mahadeva (great god) and Vishvanath (universal lord).

His consort is Parvati, the goddess of power. His two sons are Ganesha (god of good luck) and Kartikeya (god of war). His *vahan* is Nandi, the bull.

In temples, next to the Shivalinga, there is almost always an image of Nandi. But how did Nandi the bull become the vahan of Shiva? This folk-tale provides an interesting explanation.

A Vehicle for Lord Shiva

*O*ne day, lord Shiva and goddess Parvati were walking about in the jungles near Mount Kailash. As they walked, Parvati stumbled over a stone.

"Oh! My foot!" she cried.

She turned to Shiva and complained in anger, "All the gods have *vahanas* (vehicles). And you are Mahadeva – the greatest god! It's high time, you got yourself a *vahan* too."

"But, my dear, I lead the life of an ascetic. What do I need a *vahan* for?" asked Shiva.

"I'm not complaining about the way you look or the way we live. Despite your ash-covered body and matted hair, there can be none who can equal you. But it's important for a god of your level to have a vehicle. The graceful swan is Brahma's *vahan*. Vishnu has the magnificent eagle – Garuda. How majestic Indra looks when he sits astride Airavata, the elephant. A chariot drawn by radiant white-footed horses is the *vahan* of Surya. Ram is the vehicle of Agni, antelope of Vayu and buffalo of Yama. Even the goddesses have *vahans*. You are known as Pashupati – the lord of all animals – and yet you don't have a vehicle," complained Parvati.

Shiva tried reasoning with Parvati but she remained adamant. Shiva could not bear to see her upset and agreed to her wish.

'Where shall I get a *vahan* from?' wondered Shiva.

He sent a message through Sage Narad to all the gods.

"The great Lord wants to acquire a *vahan*. He has called all the gods for a meeting," informed Narad.

The gods were fearful when they received the message. "Shiva is bound to ask one of us to give him our *vahan*. He is such a powerful god. We can't even dare to say 'no' to him," worried the gods.

None of them wanted to part with their *vahans*. They pulled some excuse or the other and didn't attend the meeting.

When Shiva saw that the gods were reluctant to help, he went to the forest with Parvati and called for all the animals there. They came running as fast as they could.

"I have decided to acquire a *vahan*. Is any of you ready to take up that task?" asked Shiva.

The animals danced with joy and there were affirmations of 'take me', 'take me', 'take me', from everywhere.

A small rabbit stepped forward and said, "Please make me your *vahan*. See how soft my fur is! You'll be most comfortable riding me."

"Oh! You silly rabbit! How dare you open your mouth in front of me," roared the tiger. "I am the king of the jungle. Who else can be a better *vahan* for the great lord?"

"Get aside!" grunted the wild boar. Twitching his snout and brandishing his tusks, he said, "Please make me your *vahan*. I am strong and fierce."

"Step back you filthy fellow," growled the bear. "You don't deserve to be anyone's *vahan*. I am stronger than you. Not only will I serve the Lord as a vehicle, but will also get him sweet honey to eat."

"O lord! Please consider me too. I may be a little small, but I promise to serve you well," quipped the deer.

Like this, many animals offered to be Shiva's *vahan*. Shiva listened to all of them and said, "Please calm down. I am overwhelmed by your response. But I am finding it very difficult to choose one from amongst so many. In a few days

from now, I will give all the animals a
task to perform. Whoever completes the task
will become my *vahan*."

A bull named Nandi had been standing along with the other animals. He
was a great devotee of Shiva and was very keen to serve him. But Nandi was
very shy and had been unable to speak up in front of so many animals. When
they went away, he thought, 'I will follow Lord Shiva and speak to him alone.
I will beg and plead until he agrees to accept me as his *vahan*. This is a golden
opportunity to be of service to the Lord.' Nandi went up to Shiva, but found

him deep in conversation with Parvati. 'It will be wrong to disturb them,' thought the shy bull. He waited for the right time to approach Shiva. Every time his nerve failed him. Without eating and drinking, he stood like this for hours. The hours turned into days and still Nandi stood there. Shiva knew all along of Nandi's presence and was pleased with his devotion. He wanted to make things easy for him.

One day Nandi heard Shiva and Parvati talking.

"Have you thought of a task for the animals yet?" asked Parvati.

"Yes," answered Shiva. "Monsoons are approaching. In the middle of the rainy season, I will ask them to procure dry twigs and sticks."

"That's a good idea," agreed Parvati.

When Nandi heard this, he immediately got into action. He collected the wood, tied it into a bundle and kept it safely in a cave.

When the rains started, Shiva called the animals. They came eagerly, but were crestfallen when they heard what they had to do.

"There is water everywhere. How can we get dry twigs?" asked the rabbit.

"Everything in this forest is wet. What a tough task!" commented the deer.

"I don't think anyone can fulfil this condition," proclaimed the boar.

"An impossible job!" agreed the bear.

Nandi promptly went to the cave where he had hidden the wood. He brought the bundle and quietly placed it at Shiva's feet.

Shiva blessed Nandi and made him his *vahan*.

Shiva is worshipped in the form of a linga. The night Shiva first manifested himself in this form is celebrated as **Shivratri**. *On this day, in the month of Phalguna (around February-March), devotees fast the whole day and pray to the lord to bless them with a boon.*

SARASVATI

*S*arasvati is the goddess of knowledge, science and arts. She is represented as a fair complexioned, graceful woman with four arms. She holds the *veena* (a stringed musical instrument) with two hands, a string of pearls in the third and a book in the fourth.

The *veena* represents the fine arts, the rosary of pearls represents the spiritual sciences, and the book represents knowledge. Her dazzling white clothes and complexion represent the power of purity. She is seated on a beautiful lotus.

Her consort is Lord Brahma, the creator. Hence Sarasvati is also known as the mother of all creation. Her *vahan* is the peacock, but sometimes she is also shown riding a swan.

She is also known as Sharda (giver of essence), Vagishvari (mistress of speech), Brahmi (wife of Brahma) and Mahavidya (supreme knowledge).

Sarasvati, which literally means the 'flowing one', is also revered as a river. There is a very interesting tale as to how goddess Sarasvati became a river.

How did Sarasvati Become a River?

*L*ong, long ago, longer than you can even imagine, Lord Vishnu had three wives – Lakshmi, Ganga and Sarasvati. Vishnu was a fair god and treated all his wives well. He gave them equal attention and there were no favourites. They were all living happily, till Sarasvati started doubting Vishnu.

'Lord Vishnu is forever favouring that Ganga,' thought Sarasvati. 'He hardly pays any attention to me.'

These doubts led to resentment and jealousy towards Ganga. For small little matters, Sarasvati started picking quarrels with Ganga.

Lakshmi was often a witness to the childish conduct of Sarasvati. One day while Sarasvati was insulting Ganga, Lakshmi intervened, "You are unnecessarily doubting Ganga. This undignified behaviour of yours spoils the atmosphere of the house. Learn to be a bit more polite!"

Sarasvati was in no mood to listen. "Stop your lecture," she retorted. "I know your nature very well. You always take that Ganga's side! You two have joined hands against me. I know you don't like me!"

Lakshmi was taken aback and tried to clear the misunderstanding.

"I don't favour anyone," she explained, "I just want all of us to live happily and in peace…"

"Keep quiet!" said Sarasvati sharply before Lakshmi could even finish what she was saying. "Don't interfere in matters that don't concern you."

Despite Sarasvati's unkind words, Lakshmi remained cool and calm. But Ganga, who had been silent so far, could take it no more.

"Sarasvati!" exclaimed Ganga. "Watch your tongue! Lakshmi is trying to make you see reason in such a gentle and polite manner. And just look at yourself! You are snapping and shouting at her. Shame on you!"

Sarasvati's eyes blazed with fury. In a high-pitched voice she shouted, "You think you two can just gang up against me! Don't think I am defenceless. O.K.! Ganga, I am fed up of you and your scheming nature. You are forever fluttering around the Lord and hence he has no time to give to me."

Ganga was angry, very very angry.

"How dare you accuse me like this," she shouted.

"I can dare to do much more," retaliated Sarasvati. "Let me settle this matter once and for all. I curse you – Go! Become a river."

"Oh, ho… ho…So, I should become a river! You taunt me, you insult me and now you have cursed me! You think you are the only one who knows how to pronounce a curse. By the powers that I have acquired, I hereby curse you too – Go and become a river."

Lord Vishnu was busy conducting the affairs of the world, when he heard the raised voices. He arrived on the scene and enquired, "What is going on here?"

Ganga and Sarasvati bombarded Vishnu with their complaints against each other. Lakshmi stood quietly without uttering a single word. When Vishnu came to know all that had transpired, he was unhappy, very very unhappy. Once Ganga and Sarasvati had said all that they had to say, the enormity of the situation dawned on them.

"We are very sorry," they apologised, "We cursed each other in a moment of anger. We didn't really mean to harm each other."

"Bickering and fighting never solves anything. It only complicates matters as you can see. One must think before speaking," said Vishnu gravely.

"We don't want to become rivers," they pleaded. "Please help us."

Vishnu expressed his helplessness and said, "What can I do? You two have brought this upon yourself. If powers are not used properly, they can prove to be dangerous. Ganga, by half of your attributes you will

descend to earth as a river. Bhagirath, the great great grandson of King Sagara, will undergo severe penance and will bring you down from heaven. By the other half of your attributes, you will remain on Lord Shiva's head. Sarasvati! You are the root cause of this problem. By half your attributes, you will flow on earth as a river. By the other half of your attributes, you will from now, be the wife of Lord Brahma. As for Lakshmi, she has always remained calm and composed. She doesn't quarrel like the two of you. Hence, she alone will remain with me as my wife."

"We promise never to fight. Please forgive us and find a way out of this mess," requested Sarasvati and Ganga.

Vishnu was moved by their plight.

"I can't change the curse, but I can make it a little less severe. I hereby declare that as rivers you will both be held sacred. Your waters will be used for religious ceremonies and sacrifices. You will be considered so holy that in order to wash away their sins, people will come from afar to take a dip in your waters. Devotees will pray to you the way they pray to any other god or goddess," announced Vishnu.

Ganga and Sarasvati accepted their fate. Ever since, they have been rivers.

*In the month of Magh (around January – February) is observed a festival called **Vasant Panchami**. It is celebrated in honour of Goddess Sarasvati. In order to seek the blessings of the goddess, devotees pray to her and keep books, musical instruments and paint brushes in front of her image. In the state of Bengal, clay idols of Sarasvati are worshipped, taken out in a procession and finally immersed in the river.*

LAKSHMI

$\mathcal{L}$akshmi is the goddess of wealth, fortune and beauty. She is described as a beautiful woman standing on a lotus. She has four arms and wears a garland of unfading flowers around her neck. In two hands, she holds lotus flowers. With the third hand, she bestows gold coins and with the fourth, she blesses the worshipper.

According to the Puranas, she was incarnated as the daughter of Sage Bhrigu and his wife Khyati. She was later born out of the Kshirsagar when it was churned for nectar. As she arose from the ocean, heavenly elephants poured pitchers full of water on her.

Lakshmi's consort is Vishnu, the preserver. Whenever Lord Vishnu took a human incarnation, Lakshmi too was born as his spouse. When Vishnu was Vamana, Lakshmi was Padma; when he was Parasurama, she was Dharani; when he was Rama, she was Sita and when he was Krishna, she was Rukmini. Her *vahan* is the owl.

She is also known as Haripriya (beloved of Hari), Jaladhija (ocean born) and Lokamata (mother of the world).

Lakshmi had an elder sister named Jyeshtha, also known as Daridra. She, too, was born during the churning of the ocean, but by nature was absolutely the opposite of Lakshmi. While Lakshmi bestowed fortune, Jyeshtha bestowed misfortune and bad luck. Here is an interesting folk-tale about the two sisters.

29

A Pole Full of Gold Coins

*O*ne day Jyeshtha visited Lakshmi and complained, "I am more beautiful and more powerful than you. Yet, you are the one who always gets the respect and honour. You are the one who everyone prays to. No one bothers about me! If I go somewhere, people start looking uncomfortable and unhappy."

Lakshmi smiled and replied, "Dear sister, respect can't be commanded; it has to be earned. Being beautiful or being a relative is also not the right criterion to win someone's respect."

"Well, then what is?" asked Jyeshtha with irritation.

"Being kind and having a generous nature, I spread wealth and happiness, wherever I go. Out of gratitude, people sing my praises and want me to stay with them for longer. You, on the other hand, spread poverty, disease and misfortune. If you really want to be respected, then for once, try and spread happiness," suggested Lakshmi.

"What stuff and nonsense!" exclaimed Jyeshtha. "All this attention that you have been getting has gone to your head. My powers are stronger than yours."

Lakshmi smiled when she heard the arrogant words. This angered Jyeshtha no end and she cried, "If you have the power to turn an ordinary person into a millionaire, then I have the power to turn the same millionaire into a beggar, and that too in a matter of a few minutes."

"Really?" asked Lakshmi.

"Yes, and stop being condescending! A few kilometres from here is a small village called Haripur wherein lives a brahman named Parmanand. Let's try our powers on him. That will settle the matter once and for all."

Lakshmi accepted her sister's challenge. Dressed like village women in simple cotton sarees, the two sisters reached Haripur.

Holding a *kamandal* (small drinking vessel) in his hand, Parmanand was on his way back from the Vishnu temple.

Jyeshtha spotted him and remarked, "Lakshmi, your chance first. Help him whichever way you can!"

There was a bamboo pole lying on the path. Lakshmi snapped her fingers. Immediately, the pole filled up with gold coins. Parmanand spotted the pole and said, "Oh! What a sturdy thing. It will definitely come in handy." He tucked the pole under his arm and started walking.

"My turn now," announced Jyeshtha.

Just then a young boy came running towards Parmanand. "Hello Mangal! Where are you off to?" asked Parmanand.

"My grandfather is making a new charpoy (stringed cot) for me. He has asked me to get a long and narrow piece of wood for the same," replied Mangal.

"Uncle, that's a lovely pole you have. It's exactly what I am looking for. Will you sell it to me? Please, Please."

"All right," replied Parmanand.

"Uncle, this five-rupee coin is all that I have right now. Will it do?" asked Mangal.

Parmanand took the coin and gave Mangal the pole. He dropped the coin in his *kamandal* and walked on.

Jyeshtha looked at Lakshmi meaningfully and mocked, "A pole full of gold coins sold for five rupees! But I'm not through with him yet. Just wait and watch. Ha!"

As Parmanand came near the village pond, he saw lovely pink lotuses blooming in the water. 'I'll string these flowers into a garland and offer it in the temple in the evening,' he thought. Keeping his *kamandal* under a tree and hitching up his *dhoti*, he waded into the water. A young seven-year-old boy was grazing his goat nearby. He saw the five-rupee coin shining in the *kamandal*. He looked around stealthily. Parmanand had his back towards the boy and was knee-deep in the muddy pond. The boy quickly pocketed the coin and ran off. Parmanand returned with an armful of lotuses and started on his way back home.

Jyeshtha laughed wickedly, "Ha! Ha! Ha! Ho! Ho! Ho!" Lakshmi just smiled.

Parmanand was about to enter his hut, when Mangal came rushing by. "Uncle, this pole will not do. Grandfather says that it's much too heavy to be used for a charpoy. Could you kindly return my coin?"

Parmanand took back the pole and peered in the *kamandal*, only to find it empty. "I seem to have dropped the coin somewhere," he said apologetically. "Can you come and take it some……."

Parmanand had not even completed what he was saying when a man walked up to him, pulling a little boy by his ear. "Here is your five-rupee coin," he said returning the coin to Parmanand. "This son of mine is turning into a real rascal. He pick-pocketed your money so that he could buy ice lollies. I've boxed his ears real hard. Sorry for what happened."

"Don't be too harsh on him," said Parmanand as he returned the coin to Mangal. After they had left, Parmanand picked up the pole. "It sure is heavy. It'll be ideal as a beam in my roof. The old one has nearly worn off."

Jyeshtha was chagrined by the unexpected turn of events. Lakshmi continued to smile.

"I won't let Lakshmi win. I am more powerful. I'll kill that brahman if I have to, but I will not lose," raged Jyeshtha. She clenched her fist in anger, waved her hand wildly in the air and within seconds turned into a long, black snake. With a loud hiss, she made off towards Parmanand.

The poor brahman froze with fear when he saw the deadly reptile. The snake's tongue flickered in and out as it raised its hood to strike Parmanand. Just then, Parmanand remembered the pole in his hand. Using all his strength, he brought it down hard on the snake. CRACK! The pole broke into two and the gold coins spilled out. Writhing with pain, the snake slithered away into some bushes.

Parmanand's mouth fell open. Wide eyed with shock, he goggled at the booty that lay in front of him.

Lakshmi quietly walked up to Jyeshtha who was nursing her bruises with a downcast face. She comforted Jyeshtha and said, "*Didi*, I know you are feeling bad. But do accept the fact now that true happiness comes from giving, be it wealth or love. A person who only believes in taking and making others miserable can never be happy."

Hurt and humbled, Jyeshtha kept quiet.

*During the festival of **Diwali**, prayers are offered to Goddess Lakshmi. It is a common belief that Lakshmi and Jyeshtha have a pact that if one of them is present in somebody's house, the other will not enter. Jyeshtha loves squalor and dirt while Lakshmi likes just the opposite. In order to welcome Lakshmi on Diwali, special efforts are made to clean, illuminate and decorate the homes.*

PARVATI

$\mathcal{P}$arvati is the goddess of power and the consort of Lord Shiva. However, she is worshipped in her own right and not merely as the consort of Shiva.

She is depicted as fair and beautiful with two arms. In one hand, she holds a blue lotus and with the other hand she blesses her devotees. Her image is always to be found along with the *shivlinga* in temples.

She was married to Shiva not once, but twice. As daughter of King Daksha and wife of Shiva, she immolated herself in the fire when her father insulted her husband. When she was reborn as Uma to Himavan and Mena, she again married Shiva.

Her manifestation as Durga is very popular. Sitting astride a ferocious lion and armed with numerous weapons, Durga and her various other forms destroyed demons like Durg, Raktbeej, Chand, Mund, Mahishasur, Dhumralochana, Shumbh and Nishumbh.

Parvati is also known as Jagaddhatri (mother of the world), Annapurna (bestower of food), Ganeshjanani (mother of Ganesha), Gauri (the white one) and Aparajita (the invincible).

It is often seen that whenever one is in trouble, one turns to god. Something similar happened to a poverty-stricken brahman. A devotee of goddess Parvati, he prayed to her ardently. Were his prayers answered? Did the goddess help him?

The Magic Pots

*I*n a tiny village lived a poor brahman named Rasik Lal. Whatever alms he brought home were barely enough to support him and his family. Often his wife and children had to go without food. To take care of the needs of his family, Rasik Lal used to borrow money from Baiju – a shrewd moneylender. Since he never had enough to pay back, the principle and the accumulated interest was now a hefty amount. However, Rasik Lal and his wife Ratna were great devotees of Goddess Parvati. Every day, without fail, they went to the temple and prayed to her.

The past few days had been especially tough for Rasik Lal. The wails of his young daughter rang in his ears as she cried for food. "The children are very hungry. I had gone to Baiju for some loan but he has refused to give us more till we clear the old dues. I don't know what to do. Can you please go to the forest and pluck some wild fruits and berries?" requested Ratna.

With a heavy heart, Rasik Lal walked to the forest. He sat under an old banyan tree and cried in anguish, "Oh Mother Goddess, have pity on this devotee of yours. I can't bear to see the plight of my children!"

There was a blaze of light and Goddess Parvati appeared before him. Rasik Lal was dazzled by her brilliance. He folded his hands and then fell at her feet.

"Rasik Lal, rise," said the goddess. "I am very happy with your devotion." She snapped her fingers and lo, an earthen pot appeared in her hands. "Take this pot Rasik Lal, turn it around thrice and say: JAI DURGE! JAI PARVATI! You will never be short of money."

Before Rasik Lal could thank her, the goddess had disappeared. Rasik Lal followed the instructions given by the goddess. CATANK! There was a sudden

flash and something clanked in the pot. Gingerly, Rasik Lal put in his hand, and took out the contents. A dozen silver coins gleamed in the palm of his hand. Rasik Lal gasped. He thanked Goddess Parvati and started walking back to his village.

On the way, he crossed the moneylender's house. 'Baiju is forever pestering me to return the money I owe him. Why don't I clear my debt with this money and then go home – a free and happy man?'

As soon as Baiju saw Rasik Lal he rasped, "Don't you dare ask me for more mon…"

"I have actually come to repay you," said Rasik Lal and gave him the twelve silver coins.

'How did he manage that?' wondered Baiju, as he stroked his chin.

"Hmmm… But this is not enough! To clear all that you owe me, you'll have to give me ten, no, twelve more silver coins," said Baiju.

"All right. I'll give you twelve coins."

"And how do you propose to do that?" asked Baiju as he narrowed his eyes and looked intently at the pot Rasik Lal was clutching.

"With the blessings of Goddess Parvati," replied Rasik Lal calmly.

Intrigued, Rasik Lal coaxed and cajoled, till Rasik Lal told him how to use the pot. The sly moneylender delayed Rasik Lal's departure on some pretext or the other, and seizing an opportune moment, exchanged the magic pot with an ordinary one. Unaware of what had transpired, Rasik Lal went home. With great joy he narrated his encounter with Goddess Parvati to his wife.

"We are indeed blessed that the goddess appeared in person before you," said Ratna.

"Ratna, our poverty-stricken days are a thing of the past now!" exclaimed Rasik Lal drumming his fingers on the pot.

Rasik Lal held the pot carefully, turned it round thrice and said loudly: JAI DURGE! JAI PARVATI!

Nothing happened. He shouted the words, but again nothing happened.

"It worked just fine in the forest. What's happened now? The goddess had said …."

"Don't fret! What could be a more fitting reward for a devotee than seeing the goddess he worships in person."

"You are absolutely right Ratna."

Next day, after praying at the temple, Rasik Lal went to the forest again. As he neared the old banyan tree in the forest, there was a blaze of light and once again Goddess Parvati appeared.

She smiled, gave Rasik Lal another earthen pot and said, "Take this magic pot, turn it around thrice and say: JAI DURGE! JAI PARVATI! You'll never go hungry again."

Before Rasik Lal could thank her, she had disappeared. Rasik Lal followed the instructions given by the goddess. There was a sudden flash. Rasik Lal blinked when he saw the pot brimming with *rasogullas*. Carefully he placed one in his mouth. Then another, then another…. Soft, spongy and sweet, they were the best *rasogullas* he had ever eaten.

'How happy Ratna will be, when she sees this pot,' thought Rasik Lal. 'She is always complaining that there is no food in the house. I'll open a *rasogulla* shop in the village – RASIK LAL RASOGULLA SHOP.'

He tucked the pot under his arm and humming to himself, quickly made way for home. On the way, Baiju saw him and thought, 'I robbed this fellow of his magic pot yesterday and today he's singing a song! Fishy behaviour! Maybe that's another magic pot in his hand. I'd better find out!'

"My dear Rasik Lal," called out Baiju. "Why the haste? Come and have some snacks with me."

"No! No! I'm not hungry!"

"Why? Are you returning from a feast?"

"No, but I've just eaten the most delicious *rasogullas*."

"Really? I would also like to taste these wonderful *rasogullas*. I just love *rasogullas*."

Rasik Lal offered him the *rasogullas* that were left in the pot. Baiju savoured their sweet taste, and once again duped Rasik Lal by replacing his magic pot with an ordinary one.

On reaching home, Rasik Lal showed the pot to Ratna, turned it around thrice and said: JAI DURGE! JAI PARVATI!

Sure enough, nothing happened. Again and again, Rasik Lal said the magic words. Nothing happened. Rasik Lal scratched his head and thought, 'The magic pots work so well in the forest. What goes wrong when I reach home?'

Simpleton that he was, he never imagined that the moneylender was deceiving him. Next day, Rasik Lal went to the same spot in the forest. This time too Parvati appeared. She gave him yet another earthen pot and also whispered some instructions in his ear. Rasik Lal took the pot from Goddess Parvati and thanked her with folded hands.

As soon as Baiju saw him, he invited Rasik Lal inside. "So what is new and interesting about your pot today?" he enquired as he examined it.

Rasik Lal quickly said the magic words: JAI DURGE! JAI PARVATI!

There was a sudden hissing noise and black smoke started coming out of the pot. Along with the smoke, an enormous demon also soared up. He had dark black skin, a thick stocky neck and sharp curved horns on his head. In his hand he held a huge club. The demon swung the club in the air and brought it down hard on Baiju's backside. He fell down. The moment he got up, the demon gave him another blow.

"Hai! Hai! Please don't hit me," howled Baiju.

"Where are the magic pots?" thundered the demon.

Baiju scampered inside, brought out the magic pots and handed them over to Rasik Lal.

"Hoo! Hoo! Hoo! Ha! Ha! Ha! If you ever trick anyone again, I'll swallow you whole," warned the demon.

"No, no, never. Please forgive me," whispered Baiju, shivering from head to toe.

Once again there was a hissing sound and the demon disappeared into the pot. Rasik Lal took all the three pots and thanking Goddess Parvati from the core of his heart, went home.

With the help of the magic pots, Rasik Lal opened a *rasogulla* shop, which became known far and wide for its excellent sweets. Baiju started leading an honest life and never cheated anyone again.

Goddess Parvati took the form of a ten-armed beautiful woman to kill a demon named Durg. Hence she is also called Durga. To celebrate this victory, the people of West Bengal celebrate **Durga Puja***. During this ten-day long festival, an idol of Goddess Durga is erected and various cultural programmes are held. On the tenth day, which is also Dussehra, the idol is immersed in the river or sea with great fanfare.*

Ganesha is worshipped as the god of good luck and the god of wisdom. His idol shows him as having a large human body and four hands. He has the head of an elephant and two tusks, one of which is broken. In one hand he holds an axe, in the second a noose, in the third a *modak* and with the fourth he blesses his devotees. He is dressed in beautiful clothes, bedecked with jewels and a snake is tied around his huge belly.

Ganesha is the master of all arts and sciences. It is customary to worship Ganesha before starting any important activity or ceremony.

The elder son of Lord Shiva and Parvati, various myths and legends are associated with his birth and also with his broken tusk. According to a popular belief, Ganesha was created out of the scurf from Parvati's body. As per another belief, Ganesha wrote the epic Mahabharata, while sage Veda Vyaas recited it.

Ganesha's two wives are Riddhi (prosperity) and Siddhi (success). His *vahan* is a *mushak* (mouse).

He is also known as Vighneshwara (lord of obstacles), Vinayaka (supreme leader), Gajanana (elephant-faced) and Ganapati (lord of all beings).

Ganesha had a brother called Kartikeya (lord of war). The two brothers were very close and almost inseparable. A mischievous sage was jealous of their unity. He asked his friend to create conflict between them. Did the duo succeed?

The Golden Lotus

Narad was the chief messenger of the gods. Though a wise and learned sage, he had a terrible vice – he was a mischief-monger to the hilt. He often created situations which would cause misunderstandings amongst people. When they quarrelled, he felt happy at his handiwork.

One day, while he was wandering around, he met Kantakmukhi–an old acquaintance of his. An *apsara* from heaven, Kantakmukhi had one thing in common with Narad – she too loved to create trouble and problems for others.

"Oh my dear friend Narad, how are you?" said Kantakmukhi with a smile on her face.

Narad greeted her and soon they were engrossed in a hearty talk. Amid peals of laughter, Kantakmukhi narrated incident after incident of her craftiness. Not to be left behind, Narad too described his misdoings with equal gusto.

"I am the best amongst the best in the art of mischief-making," announced Kantakmukhi proudly.

In the distance Narad could see Ganesha and Kartikeya approaching. With their fingers interlocked, the two brothers walked along merrily.

"Let's put your prowess to test," suggested Narad. "If you are really as good as you proclaim, then make these sons of Shiva quarrel with each other."

Kantakmukhi readily took up the challenge. She dived into a nearby lake and transformed herself into a beautiful lotus.

As Ganesha and Kartikeya came closer to the lake, they spotted the lotus. So exquisite was the flower that they both wanted it. The lotus was golden in colour, and each and every petal sparkled and gleamed in the sun. As they stared in wonder at its beauty, the lotus spoke up, "I have been created specially for the son of Shiva and Parvati."

Ganesha quickly plucked the flower and said, "The golden lotus belongs to me."

"You heard what it said. The lotus has been created for the son of Shiva and Parvati. You are no real son. You were created out of the scurf of my mother's body," retorted Kartikeya snatching the lotus from Ganesha's hand.

"Watch your tongue or else I'll pull it out," replied Ganesha in anger.

Hidden behind some trees, Narad was enjoying himself. 'Clever Kantakmukhi,' thought Narad. 'I have never been able to create discord between these brothers. But look at them squabbling now!'

Kartikeya clenched his fist to box Ganesha. But Ganesha was too quick. He wrapped his trunk around Kartikeya, lifted him high up in the air and then threw him down. Now Kartikeya was not an ordinary god, but the god of war. He quickly got to his feet and pulled out his spear. Ganesha took out his axe and the two stood glowering at each other.

Narad panicked. What had started as a minor altercation had taken a nasty turn. If either of them got hurt, Shiva's wrath would know no bounds. Narad shuddered when he thought of what might happen if he were to become the object of that fury.

Narad rushed forward and stood between them. "Stop, both of you!" he cried. "Is this the way to settle an argument? Why don't you set a condition? The one who will fulfil it first can take the golden lotus."

Both Ganesha and Kartikeya agreed that it was a wise suggestion.

"Whoever takes three rounds of the world first will be entitled to the golden lotus," said Kartikeya. "Do you agree Ganesha?"

Ganesha nodded. Kartikeya's *vahan* was the peacock. He immediately mounted it and took off.

'My peacock is so swift,' thought Kartikeya, patting the neck of the bird. 'By the time that pot-bellied brother of mine climbs on to that little mouse of his, I would have completed one round. The golden lotus is sure to be mine.'

Ganesha, in the meantime, mounted his *mushak* and slowly made way to where his parents were. Shiva and Parvati were seated on the cliff of a mountain when Ganesha approached them. He folded his hands and bowed before them. Then he took three rounds of the mountain and sat down to snack on some *modaks*.

A few hours later, Kartikeya arrived. Huffing, puffing and sweating, he shouted, "I've done it! I've done it! I've completed the rounds! I've completed the rounds! I'm first!"

"No I am," said Ganesha, coolly popping another *modak* in his mouth.

"You are busy eating sweets and you say you're the first to complete the condition. How is it possible?" asked Kartikeya.

Ganesha got up and said solemnly, "My parents are my entire world and I have circled around them thrice."

Before Kartikeya could say anything further, a voice from the skies announced, "Ganesha is the winner!"

"But you are my brother and I love you a lot. Here, keep the golden lotus," offered Ganesha.

"No, a flower is hardly worth fighting for. You have won and it rightfully belongs to you," said Kartikeya. The brothers hugged each other and Kartikeya went off.

Ganesha was the god of wisdom. He closed his eyes and soon identified the culprit responsible for the entire incident. He threw the golden lotus on the ground and chanted a special mantra. Immediately, Kantakmukhi appeared in her original form.

"You crafty woman! You mischief-monger! You wanted me to fight with my own brother! You are very fond of sowing thorns in the lives of others, aren't you? And you are also fond of turning into a plant. So be it. From now onwards you will turn into the thorny *gokhru* (bramble) bush and will grow on earth. You don't deserve a place in heaven," cursed Ganesha.

So that's how the bramble bush originated.

Life went on. Then, many many years later, Ganesha decided to meditate. For certain reasons, Indra didn't want this to happen. He sent the most beautiful

of his *apsaras* (celestial dancers) to entice him and break his concentration. The *apsaras* got to work and started dancing before him. By chance, Ganesha was seated near a clump of *gokhru* bushes. Kantakmukhi figured out what the *apsaras* were up to. She quickly spread the needle-like thorns of the *gokhru* all around Ganesha. As the *apsaras* danced, the sharp thorns pricked their feet. Groaning and moaning, they fled.

Ganesha had not opened his eyes, but the omniscient god knew that Kantakmukhi had helped him. He called her and she approached with folded hands.

"Forgive me! I regret having done what I did. People dislike the very sight of the thorny *gokhru* bush. Please have mercy on me."

"I can't undo the curse, but I can make a small change," said Ganesha. "From now on, the fruit of your bush will be used for medicinal purposes. The *gokhru* bush will always be dear to me, and during the festival of Ganesh Chaturthi, its fruit will be offered on my idol."

*Ganesha is supposed to have been born on the fourth day in the month of Bhadrapad (sometime in September). In western parts of India and especially in the state of Maharashtra, his birthday is celebrated in the form of a ten-day long festival called **Ganesh Chaturthi**. Huge idols of Ganesha are installed and for ten days various cultural events are organised. On the last day, the idol is immersed in a well, river or the sea amidst great rejoicing.*

HANUMAN

Hanuman, the monkey god, is depicted as a strong and sturdy monkey. In one hand, he holds a *gada* (mace) and in the other he holds a mountain. Famous as the devotee of Lord Rama, he is often shown sitting at the feet of Rama with his hands folded.

The son of the monkey chief Kesari and his wife Anjana, even as a baby, he was special. When he was very young, Lord Indra injured him with his *vajra*. Vayu, the wind god, saved Hanuman and nursed him back to health. He took such a liking to the mischievous little monkey that he bestowed many boons on him. As a result, Hanuman could leap as high and as far as he pleased, could assume any shape and could enter any place he wanted to. He could go without nourishment for any length of time and no weapon could ever harm him. Lord Brahma himself bestowed the last boon.

Besides being strong and powerful, Hanuman was also intelligent and learned. He had mastery over the Vedas. His heroic feats are described at length in the epic Ramayana. The most prominent amongst them is the way he uprooted an entire mountain called Dronachal and brought it to Rama. A very popular god, he is especially honoured by wrestlers. Worshipped all over India, there are innumerable shrines dedicated to him. He is also known as Sankatmochan (remover of difficulties) and Pawanputra (wind's son).

But who was Hanuman? Was he a mere monkey blessed with special powers? Or is there more to it? It is widely belived that Hanuman was an incarnation of Lord Shiva. But this legend explores an altogether different possibility.

50

The Face in the Mirror

A great sage named Narad was the messenger of the gods. He roamed the three worlds, passing information from one to the other. Narad was a great devotee of Lord Vishnu. So great was his devotion that whenever he greeted someone, it was with the words 'Narayan! Narayan!' The words were characteristic of him. Whoever heard them, could safely predict that Narad was in his midst, without even bothering to look up. (Narayan is another name for Lord Vishnu)

Narad was a greater orator and an even greater musician; besides, he was very, very handsome. With the passage of time Narad's vanity regarding his looks increased and so did his arrogance. Once, a *gandharva* (celestial singer in heaven) said to him, "Oh Narad, I attended a wedding recently. The groom was ever so handsome."

"Stuff and nonsense! No one can be more handsome than me. I just have to smile and all the *apsaras* come running to me," pronounced Narad haughtily. Grinning sheepishly, he said in a conspiring sort of manner, "You know what, any maiden in the three worlds would be more than happy to marry me."

Then with a smirk on his face and his nose in the air, Narad walked off. Unknown to him, Goddess Lakshmi (consort of Vishnu) had overheard the entire conversation. She went to Vishnu and reported Narad's arrogance to him.

Vishnu smiled and said, "So much vanity is never good for anyone and especially not for a holy person."

"Lord, I know just the right way to humble Narad," beamed Lakshmi.

Vishnu heard her out and agreed to her plan. Lakshmi had already chosen an appropriate site on earth where the plan was to be executed. Lord Vishnu closed his eyes and within minutes, a magnificent kingdom came up. The royal palace with its gold pillars, intricately carved ceilings and lavish interiors was the cynosure of all eyes. Lakshmi transformed herself into a royal princess. News spread about the splendid kingdom and the ravishingly beautiful princess who lived there. When the monarch of this new kingdom announced a *swayamvar* (a ceremony carried out in the olden days, wherein a princess chose the one she wanted to marry from amongst many suitors), people seemed to have nothing else to talk about.

"The man who marries the princess will be very lucky indeed," said one.

"Yes, Princess Roopkumari is no doubt the most beautiful woman on this entire earth," concurred the second.

"Why earth? Even an *apsara* from heaven would pale in comparison!" exclaimed another.

"Not only is she pretty but also very wealthy. She is the sole heir to this majestic kingdom."

News of the *swayamvar* reached Narad as well and he decided to attend it. 'The minute Princess Roopkumari looks at me, she'll forget everyone else present there,' thought Narad.

On the appointed day and time, Narad reached the hall where the *swayamvar* was being conducted. Elephants stood at the main gate and trumpeted loudly to welcome the illustrious guests. The main hall had been beautifully decorated with colourful buntings, and the air was fragrant with the smell of fresh rose petals.

Narad took his designated place and waited for the princess to arrive. Holding a garland of sweet-smelling flowers and dressed in a golden red saree, Princess Roopkumari appeared. So stunning did she look that there was a collective gasp from everyone present. She walked with delicate and graceful

steps towards Narad. He puffed up his chest and stepped a bit forward. But to his utter astonishment, she walked right past and garlanded a dark complexioned ordinary looking person.

Narad's vanity could not bear this slight. He went up to the princess and cried out, "I am the most handsome man here and yet you chose this ordinary looking creature. Maybe you didn't see me properly. Come on, quickly garland me."

The princess looked at Narad and giggled, "Why should I marry a monkey like you?"

"What! You dare call me – the most handsome man in this world – a monkey? Are you not feeling all right?"

"Have you seen yourself in the mirror lately?" asked Roopkumari trying hard to suppress her smile.

Taken aback, Narad immediately took out a hand mirror and peered at it. A red, hairy, bulbous and big-toothed face, very much like that of a monkey,

stared back at him. Narad screamed in anger and smashed the mirror to the ground.

Narad glowered at the princess and her groom, and clenched his fists. "You two are somehow responsible for this and I curse you both. The way you have separated me from my handsome self, similarly you will also be separated from each other."

Immediately, the princess and her groom took their true forms. And Narad found himself facing Vishnu and Lakshmi. The make-believe kingdom and all the people in it disappeared.

Narad's jaw fell open when he saw the god and goddess. He fell at their feet with tears of remorse running down his cheeks. "Please forgive me," he begged. "In my arrogance, I have pronounced a curse on my lord and master. Please forgive me! I never meant to do so. My life will not be worth living if you have to suffer on my account."

Unruffled as ever, Vishnu smiled benignly, "It was important for you to learn this lesson. And as far as your curse goes, it will have effect. We will be born as Rama and Sita and will be separated from each other."

"Oh lord, please don't punish your humble servant like this. I'll happily remain a monkey forever but I can't bear to be away from you. To atone for the sin of having cursed you, allow me to serve you for the rest of my life," sobbed Narad.

Vishnu wiped away Narad's tears and said, "Don't fret Narad. This human incarnation of mine as Rama is necessary for the welfare of the people on earth. But at the same time, your monkey form will also be an invaluable aid to us. As Hanuman—the monkey god, You will be instrumental in re-uniting Rama and Sita."

Thus Narad, a devotee of Lord Vishnu, was reborn as Hanuman, a devotee of Lord Rama.

The full moon day in the month of Chaitra (around March and April) is celebrated as **Hanuman Jayanti.** *In keeping with the belief that Hanuman was born on this day, devotees keep a fast and offer special prayers at his temple. Tuesdays are especially associated with Hanuman. Devotees offer bundi (special sweets made of gram flour) to his idol and also recite the Hanuman Chaalisa – an ode dedicated to Hanuman. It's believed that the ones who recite it regularly shall face no difficulties in life.*

INDRA

Indra is the god of heaven and the protector of the eastern direction. He controls rain, thunder and also lightning. Since rainfall is important for the sustenance of life on earth, he was worshipped widely, especially in the Vedic age. Many hymns in the Vedas are dedicated to Indra.

Indra is described as having four hands. In two hands, he holds a lance and in the third a thunderbolt. His fourth hand is empty.

He is said to be the son of Heaven and Earth and the twin brother of Agni (god of fire). His consort is Indrani, also called Sachi. Indra's vehicle is a majestic white elephant named Airavata. This elephant emerged from the Kshirsagar during the churning of the ocean.

Indra lives on Mount Meru, in a beautiful city called Amravati. Replete with landscaped gardens, diamond-studded pillars and dancing *apsaras*, this city was built by Vishvakarma (the architect of the gods).

Indra is also known as Divapati (lord of gods), Bajri (he who wields a thunderbolt), and Swargapati (lord of heavens).

Once a mighty demon named Vrittasura created havoc on earth and in heaven. Indra fought a long battle with this demon. Many gods and a well-known saint came forward to help.

Battle and Sacrifice

*O*nce there lived a three-headed sage called Vishwaroop. With one head, Vishwaroop only read the Vedas, and had mastered them. He was also a great ascetic and spent hours in meditation. He had thus acquired a lot of strength and powers. His father was a renowned sage named Twashta, but his mother was a demon.

Indra, the god of heaven, was getting worried about Vishwaroop's progress. 'With each passing day, Vishwaroop is getting more and more powerful. There will soon come a time when his power will surpass mine. He will surely defeat me and usurp my crown,' thought a worried Indra. 'I'd better do something to stop him!'

He sent beautiful *apsaras* (dancing nymphs) from his court to disrupt the sage's meditation. The *apsaras* danced and danced but could not break Vishwaroop's concentration. They returned to Indra and reported, "We tried our level best to entice that sage but all our efforts were in vain."

Indra tried other tactics as well but none of them were successful. He was paranoid and started getting nightmares of being dethroned and made captive. 'Vishwaroop may be a brahman, but his maternal uncles are demons. If he comes into power, the demons will get a strong foothold of heaven,' thought Indra.

Indra worried and worried. Finally he grew so desperate that killing Vishwaroop appeared to be the only solution to his problem. Pretty sure that he was doing the right thing, Indra approached Vishwaroop and with his *vajra* sliced off the brahman's head.

On hearing of his son's death, Twashta was filled with anger. "Indra has killed my innocent son!" he cried. "I will not let him go unpunished for a crime like this!"

Twashta performed a great sacrifice. He went without food, water and sleep, and concentrated only on the sacrifice. After eight days and nights, he pulled out a hair from his head and flung it into the sacrificial fire. The hair sizzled and from the bright orange flames stepped out an enormous demon. Twashta named him Vrittasur. The demon was as bright as the fire from which he had emergved and was so huge that his head touched the sky.

"Son, I have created you so that you can avenge your brother's death. Go, find that wily Indra and finish him off," commanded Twashta.

Vrittasur bowed before his father and went off in search of Indra. The two fought and fought but finally Vrittasur got the better of Indra. He opened his mouth wide and in one gulp swallowed Indra whole. The other gods fled in panic. They found a safe hiding place and held a meeting.

"Whatever shall we do?" said one. "Lord Indra is the king of heaven! We have to rescue him."

"I have an idea," said another god. "Let's make Vrittasur yawn. As he opens his mouth, Lord Indra can quickly hop out."

"It might just work," agreed the other gods.

The gods combined their power and cast a spell on Vrittasur. (And lo, the first yawn was created!). As the demon yawned, Indra took advantage of the opportunity. He contracted his body and jumped out of Vrittasur's stomach as fast as he could. Once on firm land, he ran for dear life.

Vrittasur reported the situation to Twashta and said, "That Indra is craftier than I thought. Father, please allow me to do penance. I want to increase my powers. Then, once and for all, I will finish off Indra."

For hundreds of years, Vrittasur sat on top of a mountain and prayed. He prayed and prayed. Finally Lord Brahma appeared and said, "Vrittasur, I grant you the boon you seek. From now on, weapons made of wood and metal will not be able to harm you."

When Indra came to know about the boon, he was more worried than ever. He went straight to Lord Vishnu and asked for his help. Lord Vishnu looked at his agonised face and said, "Don't despair Indra! There is a way out but it requires a great sacrifice, a very great sacrifice."

"What is it?' asked Indra anxiously.

"A *vajra* (thunderbolt) made from the bones of Sage Dadhichi can finish off Vrittasur."

Indra was stupefied. "Why only Sage Dadhichi's bones?" he asked.

"Ah! There's a very good reason for that. Do you remember the time the demons were threatening the gods and you had to take help from the kshatriya king Kshuva?" enquired Indra.

"Of course I remember," said Indra. "I had even given him my *vajra* to fight with."

"Yes and that's the reason Dadhichi's bones are so strong. Sage Dadhichi and king Kshuva were childhood friends. Led by Kshuva, the gods battled against the demons. Heady with victory, Kshuva went to meet Dadhichi after the battle was over. In the course of their conversation, they got into an argument. Kshuva claimed that kshatriyas were more superior than brahmans while Dadhichi insisted on the exact opposite. Neither was ready to go back on their stand and the argument turned into a fight. Dadhichi clenched his fist and landed a blow on Kshuva's head. Enraged, Kshuva took out your *vajra*, which

he had not yet returned. As the *vajra* struck Dadhichi, he fell down dead. But a fraction of a second before dying, he had called upon Shukracharya. A friend of Dadhichi and the guru of the demons, Shukracharya was an expert in *mrita sanjivani*-- the art of bringing the dead back to life. Using this very technique, Shukracharya managed to revive Dadhichi.

Dadhichi thanked Shukracharya and vowed never to let a thing like that happen to him again. Shukracharya suggested that Dadhichi should pray to the almighty Shiva. Dadhichi heeded the advice and did exactly that.

Pleased by his dedication, Lord Shiva granted him three boons. The first was that

he would be prosperous, the second that his bones would become as hard as the *vajra* itself and the third that he would die only when he so desired.

So strong are Dadhichi's bones that even my *chakra* (discus) and *brahmastra* (one of the most deadly weapons of those times) can do him no harm," explained Vishnu.

After listening to Vishnu's account, Indra, accompanied by the other gods, reached Dadhichi's hermitage. Words failed him and with folded hands, he stood quietly in front of the sage, who was deep in meditation.

Dadhichi opened his eyes and said, "Welcome Indra, I know that you have come here on the advice of Lord Vishnu. Don't worry. Your wish will be fulfilled. My bones could not have found a better use. Victory shall be thine!"

The gods stared in disbelief as without a moment's hesitation, Dadhichi closed his eyes and breathed his last. The gods bent down and oblated in front of the great sage, whose sacrifice had surpassed the greatest of all sacrifices.

Indra then called Vishwakarma, the architect of gods. Using Dadhichi's bones, he crafted a special *vajra* and handed it to Indra. Armed with the weapon, Indra went in search of Vrittasur, who had by then usurped the whole of heaven. A mighty battle ensued but finally, with the help of the *vajra*, Indra managed to slay Vritttasur.

Indra Jatra, also called the 'festival of Indra' is celebrated with great enthusiasm in Kathmandu, Nepal. Dedicated to Lord Indra, this festival is celebrated for eight days in the month of August or September. A tall wooden pole representing Indra is put up in the city square. A spectacular procession passes through the streets of Kathmandu. Amidst merry making, singing and the beating of drums, masked dancers enthral the onlookers.

SURYA

Surya is the Sun God. He is also the protector of the southwest direction. The light and energy that the sun provides is essential for the sustenance of life. Hence he is widely worshipped. The famous 'Gayatri Mantra' is also dedicated to the sun.

Surya is described as a three-eyed and four-armed man who radiates brilliance. In two hands, he holds water lilies, with the third he blesses his devotees and with the fourth he encourages them. His eyes, hands and even his tongue are golden in colour.

He is the son of Sage Kashyap and Aditi. Surya rides a golden chariot, which was built by Lord Brahma. The seven white mares that draw the chariot are Gayatri, Trishtupa, Jagati, Anushtupa, Pamkti, Vrihati and Ushnika. The name of the charioteer is Arun (Dawn).

Surya was married to Sangya, the daughter of Vishvakarma (architect of the gods). He had several children – Yama, Yamuna, Vaivaswata, Shani, Tapti, Savarni Manu, the two Ashwinis (Nasatya and Dasra) and Revanta.

Surya is also known as Dinkar (maker of the day), Bhaskar (creator of light), Vivaswat (radiant one), Savitr and Pushan.

Surya and Sangya are happily married. But Sangya decides that she will not be able to bear the sun's brilliance for the rest of her life. She puts someone in her place to take care of her children and goes away. Will Surya find out?

The Duplicate Wife

"NEE..IGHHH… .NE.. EI ….GHHH….." The mares raised up their forelegs and welcomed their master.

Surya smiled as he walked up to them. He patted their heads fondly, greeted his charioteer Arun and climbed into his gleaming chariot. In a jiffy, they were off. The golden chariot streaked through the sky. Another day's work had started. Surya carried out the very important work of bringing light and brightness on earth. Birds chirped, trees swayed and men and women folded their hands to welcome the sun god. The sun god smiled warmly but continued without stopping. Timing and speed were very important, because an entire round of the earth had to be completed.

As Surya neared a forested area in heaven, he spotted a beautiful young maiden plucking flowers from a tree. He was immediately attracted to her. Next day when Surya passed that way, he saw her again. He very much wanted to talk to her and get to know her better. But he was responsible for carrying out a very important task. There would be chaos on earth if he didn't complete his round on time. Surya became sad and no longer smiled as he charged through the clouds in the sky.

Everyone noticed the change in him. Arun, his charioteer, noticed; his steeds noticed; all the other gods noticed; even the people on earth noticed. "Something is wrong," they said. "The sun is losing its warmth."

Surya's friend Vayu, the wind god, took him aside and asked him what the problem was. Surya explained the situation to him. "I want to marry that fair

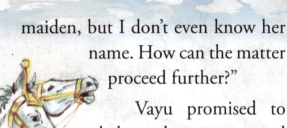

maiden, but I don't even know her name. How can the matter proceed further?"

Vayu promised to help and soon returned with the information Surya had been seeking. "The girl's name is Sangya. She is the daughter of Vishvakarma, the architect of the gods. We put forth your proposal to him and …. and…."

"And what? Tell me fast," said Surya impatiently.

"And he has agreed to the match. He also said that he couldn't have found a better son-in-law," replied Vayu.

Surya thanked Vayu and smiled after days. He smiled and smiled and smiled.

The wedding was a grand affair solemnised in the presence of many guests. Surya was a loving and caring husband and Sangya was a devoted wife. They had three children – Yama, Yamuna and Vaivaswata. Sangya was very happy with Surya, but there was one problem – she was unable to bear the sun's brilliance. Her eyes watered if she looked at him. Her mouth and throat went dry if she was near him. Her tender skin had shrivelled and was burnt from many places. Her hair, which had once been long and lustrous, was now frizzy and scorched.

Sangya was in a dilemma. She stood alone and thought out aloud, "I don't want to leave my husband and children. I love them ever so much. But I can't spend the rest of my life being roasted like this. How I long for some cool and shade! Whatever shall I do?" Her eyes welled up with tears.

"Don't despair! Everything will be O.K.," said a voice.

Sangya looked all around but there was no one present. "Who's that?" asked a startled Sangya.

"It's me, Chhaya – your shadow!"

"Oh!" exclaimed Sangya, wiping away her tears. "How will things be O.K.?"

"I'm sure you will find a solution to your problem. I will help you," offered Chhaya.

"If you really mean what you say, then I know how you can help," said Sangya excitedly.

Using some special magic, she turned Chhaya into a real person.

"You are my shadow and look exactly like me. From now on, stay with Surya and look after my children," begged Sangya.

Sangya went away to her father's house. After a few months, Vishvakarma said, "Sangya, it was lovely to see you. But it's time you returned to your husband and children."

'It is not possible for me to stay here any longer. But if I go anywhere else, I'm sure to be recognised for who I am,' thought Sangya. So, using some more magic, she turned herself into a mare and went off to the forests to do penance.

Chhaya in the meanwhile had settled down to her new life and was enjoying every bit of it. Surya didn't suspect anything and treated Chhaya as Sangya. She also had three children from Surya – Shani, Tapti and Savarni Manu. Initially she was a good mother to Sangya's children, but gradually her feelings changed. She became unkind and harsh towards them. She didn't even feed them properly. Sangya's children were bewildered at the change in their mother but didn't know what to do.

One day Chhaya got a box of sweets and gave some to all her three children. Yama saw the sweets and his mouth watered.

"Give us also some," he requested Chhaya.

"Not today," she said sharply and put away the box.

"You never give us anything nice to eat!" retaliated Yama.

"Stop being greedy," said Chhaya.

"You are always so horrid to us!" cried Yama and stamped his foot in anger. As he did so, he accidently kicked Chhaya.

Chhaya was furious. "You silly mannerless brat! How dare you hit me! I curse you – the very foot with which you have kicked me will be devoured by insects."

As Yama cowered with fright, Yamuna tried her best to comfort him. The curse started taking effect and soon Yama's leg started paining. When he could not bear it any more, Yama went to his father and tearfully narrated all that had happened. Surya looked at the swollen foot with concern. Using his special powers, he negated the effect of the curse and comforted the frightened boy.

But the incident set him thinking, 'However much a mother may curse her child, it can never have effect on him. That means the person in my house who cursed Yama is not his mother. That also means that she is not Sangya, but an impostor. Then, where is Sangya? What has this impostor done to her?'

Surya confronted Chhaya and she blurted out the truth. Surya immediately left in search of his real wife. Not finding her at Vishvakarma's house, he sat down to meditate. Using divine powers, he found out where Sangya was.

He transformed himself into a horse and joined Sangya in the forest. Sangya was delighted to see her husband and it was a tearful re-union. They spend many months together like this. But it could not go on forever. Surya had to return to his abode and to his duties.

Vishvakarma found out about the complication in his daughter's marital life and came forward to help. "If I can reduce the sun's brilliance a bit, the problem will be solved," said Vishvakarma. "Surya, will you allow me to reshape your body?"

Surya agreed. After rubbing red sandalwood paste on his body, Vishvakarma turned him around on a lathe and sliced off one-eighth of his brilliance.

'Why waste all this brilliance,' thought Vishvakarma. He immediately got down to work and crafted some special weapons from it – a discus for Vishnu, a trident for Shiva and a lance for Kartikeya. He also made a palanquin for Kubera (the god of wealth).

Surya's altered energy level no longer hurt Sangya and he now looked handsomer than ever. After thanking her father, she happily went off home.

In the state of Orissa near the city of Puri is located the **Konark Sun Temple**. This temple is dedicated to Surya, the sun god and is a masterpiece of Orissa's medieval architecture. It is designed in the shape of a chariot carrying the sun god. A major portion of the temple is now destroyed. Originally, at the base of the temple were 24 intricately carved wheels, each about 10 feet in diameter. The spokes of these wheels served as sundials and the shadows formed by them could give the exact time of the day. Even today, tourists throng to see this majestic and unique temple.

Animal Tales from Indian Mythology
Vol. 1 & 2

Full Colour Books

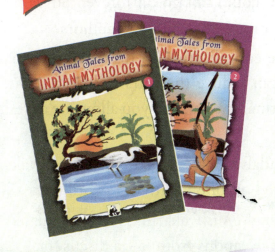

A Collection of popular Mythological stories that bring alive the feats of gods & goddesses along with their animal friends.

Have you ever wondered…
• why Ganesha has an elephant's head and only one tusk? • why Kamadhenu is called the wish fulfilling cow? • how Nandi bull became Lord Shiva's devoted vahana? • about the heartwarming story of virtuous Yudhishtra and his ever faithful dog? • how Lord Shiva is saved by Lord Vishnu & Nandi? • why Hanuman fought Makardhwaja, his own son to save Lord Rama? • how Shibi Rana saves a dying pigeon? • how Surapadama- a terrifying asura- is turned into a peacock? • about the spellbinding story of how Krishna and Balarama fight Dhenakasura? • the reason behind Sugreeva's stirring battle with Vali?

To know all this and much more, turn the pages of these books…

PANDA
Unicorn Books

PANDA

Quality reading for children...

Indian Tales & Global Tales, New Tales & Folk tales,
Fables, Legends & Mythology and Books on
growing up well, first told or retold by children's authors

9227 B • Rs. 36/-
Hindi: 9230 A • Rs. 36/-

9228 C • Rs. 36/-
Hindi: 9232 C • Rs. 36/-

9234 A • Rs. 36/-
Hindi: 9233 D • Rs. 36/-

9360 C • Rs. 96/- H.B.

9361 D • Rs. 75/-

9235 B • Rs. 60/-

9237 D • Rs. 60/-

9236 C • Rs. 60/-

9238 A • Rs. 60/-

9243 B • Rs. 75/-

9245 D • Rs. 60/-

9291 A • Rs. 50/-

9292 B • Rs. 50/-

9280 B • Rs. 50/-

9279 A • Rs. 50/-

9242 A • Rs. 75/-

9244 C • Rs. 60/-

9276 B • Rs. 75/-

9277 C • Rs. 50/-

9273 C • Rs. 75/-

9274 D • Rs. 75/-

Price: 395/-

9294 D (H.B.) Fully colour

Price: 395/-

9293 C (H.B.) Fully colour